Loving War

Eighty-Two Poems
for your Soul

Shane A. Worley

Order this book online at www.trafford.com
or email orders@trafford.com

Most Trafford titles are also available at major online book retailers.

Note for Librarians: A cataloguing record for this book is available from Library
and Archives Canada at www.collectionscanada.ca/amicus/index-e.html

Printed in Victoria, BC, Canada.

ISBN: 978-1-4269-1657-1 (Soft)
ISBN: 978-1-4269-1658-8 (Hard)

Library of Congress Control Number: 2009934680

*We at Trafford believe that it is the responsibility of us all, as both individuals
and corporations, to make choices that are environmentally and socially sound.
You, in turn, are supporting this responsible conduct each time you purchase a
Trafford book, or make use of our publishing services. To find out how you are
helping, please visit www.trafford.com/responsiblepublishing.html*

*Our mission is to efficiently provide the world's finest, most comprehensive
book publishing service, enabling every author to experience success.
To find out how to publish your book, your way, and have it available
worldwide, visit us online at www.trafford.com*

Trafford rev. 9/3/2009

 www.trafford.com

North America & international
toll-free: 1 888 232 4444 (USA & Canada)
phone: 250 383 6864 ♦ fax: 812 355 4082 ♦ email: info@trafford.com

My Definition of Poetry

A meaningful compilation of beautiful words strategically placed which are meant to subdue the inquisitive minds into feeling, witnessing, or understanding the emotions, experiences, or thoughts of the artist through the expression of beauty, rage, pain, and imagination.

Introduction

Many years ago I decided I would share what may be described as art, within my literature of poems. I began writing as much and as often as I could. Expressions of love when that was what inspired me and of the patriotic symbolism I hold dear to my heart. Many bumps in my life's road have deterred me from following through with completing this book until now. I hope that it will open your eyes for the care of that which is most sacred. Love. To remember that you are cared about and may relate in some way to the feelings of affection I have tried to portray.

I will share with you many pieces of experiences of victory and the loss of comrades as well. The brutality of battle and the consciousness of purpose for there are far too many times that the wayward lose direction in their mission. I have seen it over and over again. I am and have been a United States Marine for 8 years and enjoy the pleasures of self sacrifice for the benefit of others well-being and quality of life. It brings my heart joy to know the righteous decisions that guide my actions and words are in the path of one who is higher than I. These aspects of "Loving-War" people of all nations can relate to through transparent eyes and an open heart. I hope you all enjoy reading my book.

Special Thanks

I would like to thank all of those whom know their names that filled me with the inspirational incantations of love I would otherwise remain speechless to describe this futile emotion. C.C., S.M., A.M., E.B., S.P., A.R., H.+J. M., J.P., J.P., R.C., S.P., N.S., S., C., R.W., N.T., Y.T., M.S., M., M.C., V.S., J., J., T., M.P., H.L., A.R., C.B., N.P. my loving mother and my beautiful children Selena and Nikolas.

I would like to thank the service to which I am enlisted into. The firmness of your rules, the provisions that you provide, and the discipline that you instill allow me to become a better man and I remain remiss. U.S.M.C.

I would also like to thank my lord and savior. Without your guidance and direction steering me in the path of righteousness, I would have been lost to the winds.

Loving...
(49 poems for your heart)

A Closer Look

A touch so soft, you melt away,
I saw an Angel, this blistering day.

She appeared to float, as she walked toward me,
Not a single flaw was I able to see.

I lost my breath, and grabbed my chest.
I felt so faint and needed to rest.

But then she spoke and all had gone.
The sound of the devil was filled with wrong.

So now I know to see the heart first, or I may be surprised.
And this Angel I see may be the devil in disguise.

A New Beginning

Once, long ago I felt desire, I felt love, and I felt pain.
But then it vanished, and I haven't felt it again.

Recent eyes within my sight, are clouding my dreams.
And I flutter inside, or at least so it seems.

Thoughts in my mind, feelings within, and words from my pen.
Caused by this girl, whom I call my friend.

Perhaps it is hard, for her eyes to see.
The man that I am, and the one I could be.

Stories are told, and what seems like lies.
Cause who really knows who I am inside.

And there is a place, where no one will go.
But that is the place, I want you to know.

What we call our soul, and what makes us real.
What makes this love, I'm starting to feel.

A Painful Feeling

One look one glimpse, that's all it was;
Who knew this feeling, would turn to love.

And now I'm stuck in a world alone;
Yet by myself, my feelings have grown.

So what do I do, with this pain inside;
Continue to love, or preserve my pride.

It hurts so much I can't explain;
This feeling of Love, this feeling of Pain.

A Single Look

Close your eyes and picture a world,
Where I am your man and you are my girl.

I know that we already are,
But hurts so bad when I am so far.

You know that I Love you and that you love me.
And that we will be together, for all of eternity.

When you're looking at me and I'm looking at you,
We see that there's nothing that we wouldn't do.

To make you so happy and you'd never bore me.
And our lives are unfolding, into a beautiful Love
Story.

A Spark in Me

Drowning in terror I start to flea,
From this beautiful girl, my eyes used to see.

I'm lonely inside, and everything's dark.
But she is my light that starts from a spark.

A spark that now has begun to burn.
And holding her tight is something I yearn.

Could it be true, when I look in her eyes?
It defines the man that I am inside.

Knowing my place in this crazy world.
To cherish and care for this silly girl.

It's obvious now, where I ought to be.
Right next to her, and her next to me.

Her name is no secret, yet no one can know.
Her name is the light that makes my heart glow.

A World We Share

I picture a world, I love so much;
But this world I see, I can not touch;

It seems so close, but looks so far;
Cause this world I see, is where you are.

I'd make every touch, every kiss so real;
And give your heart, only love to feel.

Your heart beats faster and left with a chill;
You're trembling within, and can't sit still;

I'd hold you close, and never let go;
Love you so much, as you already know.

Anything

A day went by, full and fast;
The feeling I felt, I wanted to last.

Excited, heart racing, you wouldn't believe;
A thirsting on my lips, I couldn't relieve.

But I'm involved, and she is too;
But if we weren't, I'd love her through.

Yet what I feel I can't explain;
And what is happening, I wouldn't change.

I'll be content, for a little while.
Making her laugh, and watching her smile.

Awaiting

How do I explain a loss of words, a loss of sight?
The feeling of loneliness when I sleep at night.

You know who you are, the one I love.
And that we go together, like ball and glove.

My wheels are turning, getting closer to you.
Waiting I sit and wonder, what will you do?

Each second I watch, turning into a year.
But being alone is the future I fear.

To see you hurt is something I dread.
And to be without you, well, I'd rather be dead.

Awaiting a Call

I reach out with words from afar.
To tell you no matter where you are.

I'll care so much and love you through.
No matter what, you decide to do.

It hurts so much, not knowing what's true.
And not knowing what's happening, inside of you.

When papers are filed and you are alone.
It's then that you should pick up a phone.

And say you'll love me, forever more.
It's then that I'll be outside of your door.

Back to the Start

Sweat starts to pour and tears start to fall.
As I wait for her, to dial and call.

Twiddling thumbs, and a tormenting mind.
Are making it easy to pour out this rhyme.

Not from a thought or love yet again.
The pain of loneliness is what strengthens my pen.

No end does it seem, will I ever find.
A girl that would love and forever be mine.

Cherish this feeling is what I will do.
It's the only way I'll know, that what I feel is true.

Saying goodbye, I don't think I could, I don't think I can.
I want to go back, to where it all began.

My friend she was, and my friend she'll stay.
Because holding her now, I hope and I pray

Desire Inside

I see your smile, from miles away;
It warms my nights and brightens my days.

A night with you, of passion and lust;
This feeling within, becomes a must.

My heart beats faster, I can't with-hold;
But you have another life, and will leave me cold.

I'm filled to the brim, with thoughts of you;
Am filled with the question, what will you do.

A desire to hold, a desire to kiss;
And when I'm alone, it's you that I miss.

Destiny

A blistering cold and loneliness makes me shiver.
It is the thought of never again
being together.
With the one I call my love
that makes me quiver.

Blinded by a stripped control.
I no longer see her, hear her, or feel her next to me.
It causes a feverish bellow, a houndish cry.
I let it out and hope.
That all will hear, all will feel my rage.
The emptiness I see.

For I am stripped of my control.
My love, my emotions, and my heart.
I will regain strength, regain control, and
regain my lost love.
This love that has been torn apart.

Where everything feels as it was always meant to be.
Then I will have found what I have always been in search of.
My destiny.

Dreamer

Dreams are for fools, that's what they've said.
But have they ever cried, have they ever bled.

Entrusting to someone, all that they are, all that they dream.
But dreams are for fools, so they make them seem.

So I focus on the now, on the things that I see.
So I don't wonder off, where I hope to be.

Pain is down there, where dreams take you.
Smashed to pieces, or broken in two.

Open your eyes and follow your feet.
Get your head out of the clouds, and back on the street.

Aren't dreams the things that make life worth while?
How bout a kiss, how bout a smile.

I wouldn't trade, my dream for a thing,
Nor the pain that I'd feel, or the joy that they bring.

Fairy Tale

I'm starting to see with you on my mind.
Of an entire new way, to write life's rhyme.

Its starts when I'm young, and ends when we're old.
And somewhere between, "OUR" lives unfold.

The beauty of mornings, the passion of night.
As darkness does fad, and approaches the light.

We're always together, in all that we do.
With you looking at me, as I look at you.

And as we get old, we start to learn.
That this love for one another, forever will burn.

A kindling spirit within our heart.
It has pierced us both, like a knife so sharp.

We watch our children as they grow and play.
And they have children of their own, oh how I dread
that day.

But through the humor and through the laughter.
In the end we'll always live, happily ever after.

Fallen For Her

A single look into her eyes is all that it takes,
And everything inside shatters and breaks.

I try to withhold what my heart wants to give.
The love that I feel, that I need to live.

Before me now a choice to decide.
Where all of my hopes and my dreams reside.

To risk all of my doubts and risk all that I fear.
This decision before me couldn't be more clear.

Open my heart, and give all that I am.
Show her true love, I know that I can.

Will she hold back, what she feels within?
Or is it over, before we begin.

I pray to the lord, let this be the end.
Cause I now have fallen, in love with my friend.

For Always

Whisper to me a secret or two.
Cause I want you to tell me, that I Love You.

Keep me close to you, close to your heart.
Cause without you with me my life falls apart.

I've heard you once say and make a promise of mine.
That we'd be together till the end of time.

We'll someday bring to this world, a beautiful child.
After you stand next to me, and walk down that isle.

I told you I promise to love you for all of my life.
And you will then see, when you are my wife.

Forever in Love

Give me your hand and I'll give you my life.
And I'll be a truthful husband, if you're a truthful wife.

Tell me how much, to fid me of fear.
And make me forget, the things that I hear.

If you've never believed, please start with me.
I'll love you FOREVER, just wait and see.

I know inside, deep down within.
That something magnificent is starting to begin.

Just make a wish and close your eyes.
I'll love you FOREVER, if you tell me no lies.

Forget Deceit

I've closed my eyes and try to see.
Your beautiful smile looking back at me.

I see it there, in front of my face.
Then I start to wonder and stare off in space.

And up in the sky I look to a star.
And I know that there, is where we are.

So far up, within the sky.
And it is that time I begin to cry.

Because of the things that I was told.
That makes my heart feel nothing but cold.

Did you deceive me, am I to believe.
Or will you set my heart at ease.

The truth is something that I now seek.
And without the truth I feel so week.

I Love you so much and I must know.
Is it the love for another, that makes you go?

I Have Searched

In everything you say and everything you do,
Makes me fall deeper in Love with you.

Everything I show you and everything you see,
Makes you fall deeper in Love with me.

Seeing us smile, and making one another laugh,
Makes me realize that our love, forever will last.

Seeing me cry and looking so sad.
Makes you want me, want me so bad.

I have searched so far and so wide.
And I can't explain how much I Love who you are inside.

Inspiration In Me

Taunted by my dreams and deft to despair;
That these dreams I have, I'll never get to share.

So I pour out my soul to those who would read;
And all will know, the inspiration in me.

Words that I speak flutter into the air;
These words are of love, yet no one is there.

From tonight until the end of time;
I'll never run out of this love, or run out of rhyme.

The kind of love that last's forever;
And the sun never sets when we are together.

But if it should set before I go;
There's just one thing that you should know.

I wanna have you near me, before I leave;
And I'll always love you, I hope you can believe.

(I was inspired to put this piece together from the song "Inspiration"
by Chicago)

I Pray To Thee

Lord grant me the serenity that I ask of.
Grant me eternal life, with she whom I Love.

She's in my heart and on my mind.
And I know you've made her, a one of a kind.

So Lord I pray that within your pile,
of lingering prayers, you make her smile.

She means so much, I can't explain.
And I Love to hear her, call out my name.

Is it wrong of me to feel your love outweighed.
And will the debt of everlasting, by me be displayed.

So my Father, Your Son, and Holy Ghost.
I Pray to you, but her...I Love the most.

I Think, Dream, Hope Too much, I Know Not Enough

I Think of you, alone I'm left SLUMBERING.
I Think of the laughter, the smiles and LOVE.
I Dream of a time when she is his, he AWAITS.
I Dream too much perhaps, but I am DESPERATE.
I Hope reality outweighs all of my MEASURES.
I Hope the love I feel, that you do TO.
I Know that you and I will someday BE.
I Know we'll love, where ever we are TAKEN.

I SLEEP, AND WAIT

I'm Waiting to Give

Do I make you smile, and give you life?
Are you anticipating the day, when we're husband and wife?

I count the days and now I see.
That there is no place that I'd rather be.

I Love you now and I always will.
Even when our bodies forever lay still.

I've pictured a life, where we walk along.
And forever is playing, our beautiful song.

If you only knew how it is that I feel.
And all of my love, to you I'd reveal.

Show me the meaning of devoted trust.
And I'll show you the meaning of defeating lust.

For I know in my heart that there's no one I love.
So I know that I, won't even share a hug.

It's only with you that I have found peace.
And all of who I am, I'm going to release.

Ingredients For Love

You stir with the spoon of life, the ingredients of Love.
A pinch of sugar, a dash of cinnamon, and a whole lot of hugs.

Thrown together in a nice little bunch.
It was the very first glance that gave you this hunch.

That this was the recipe, you've always searched for.
And it would fill your stomach and your heart galore.

You couldn't quiet make out, this feeling at first,
Then your heart did ache, and your lips did thirst.

You needed more of this Love that you felt,
And with only a taste, your mouth starts to melt.

These subtle ingredients that I've spoken of.
Mixed in the bowl of our lives, and that's how you make Love.

It Happened

I've finally been told, and she finally had shown.
That she cares for me, and how her feelings have grown.

Astounded I am, and never before.
Has someone with me, desired to explore.

The stars, the moon, and upon this earth.
And said she was looking for me since birth.

That being with me makes her float to the sky.
And if I ever left her, that she would die.

And I can't deny, the love I have inside.
And it is her love that I've searched for far and wide.

It Will Begin

Is it really so hard, is there that much doubt.
Doesn't your heart say it's me you can't be without?

I wish I could write maybe even call, a number or two.
To hear someone tell me they miss me, and that someone is you.

As it seems so easy to write for days.
I'm still clouded, by a misty haze.

Blind to the world for I'll never be.
That man that I should, with you next to me.

One month to go, but perhaps even two.
I'll start to begin, my journey towards you.

Life Just Isn't Fair

Ten fingers ten toes.
Two eyes and a nose.
Two ears and a mind.
You listen to signs.
That points you to me.
It's then that you see.
"I", am what you need.
"I", would never leave.
Your heart I would love.
My Angel, my Dove.
Your toes and your eyes.
Your smiles and cries.
Are now yours to share.
Life just isn't fair.

Lingering Thoughts

A day is too long, I'm overcome by pain.
From a longing to hear your lips, utter out my name.

There's something you should know, but maybe you do.
I cry every night, and am surrounded with thoughts of you.

I keep coming back to the very same spot.
That wonders, if she loves me, or if she does not.

I remember a flower that you once did give.
And it is the thought of that flower that helps me to live.

Do you remember my kiss, can you feel my heart.
Cause all I feel is pain, whenever we're apart.

I miss you so much, and wish I could know.
About a decision that lingers and which way you will go.

My Friend

You are the unspeakable embodiment which defines the meaning
of friend.
You are the one I share my secrets with and my ears to
whom I lend.

I listen to your dreams, your goals and inhibition.
I share with you my thoughts, my heart and intuition.

We have experienced love, felt some pain, and shared
some tears.
But through it all, I know we'll be friends for years
and years.

Gracious, and good, beautiful and true in all that you do.
These are the qualities that I see inside of you.

Now I can say I must live with the thought in
the end.
There was a time, a day, when I fell in love with my
friend.

Never Letting Go

I contemplate the joy the sorrow.
I weep over the future and I dread tomorrow.

The day when all is lost, all is wrong.
And the chance for everlasting has left and gone.

I've seen your life in the eyes you portray.
As we share a love in a beautiful way.

It's spoken in poems and written in books.
It's shown through actions and shown through looks.

Loving you completely I know isn't bad.
And I'll never let go of a love I once had.

No Other Place

Take my ears, take this pain.
So that never again, should I hear your name.

To hear its utterance, into the wind.
Makes me hurt all over again.

So I declare to you, give me your heart.
Because it hurts so bad, when we are apart.

I see so clearly what I must do.
Let you know how much, I'm in Love with You.

I shall whisper a million times, gently enough.
Nibble on your ear, and all that sweet stuff.

I'll give you my soul, if you asked me to.
Because there is no place I'd rather be, than lying next
to you.

No Place

I closed my eyes and I try to see.
Your beautiful smile, looking back at me.

I see it there, in front of my face.
Then I start to wonder and stare off into space.

Skin so soft that feels like cotton,
Makes me weep when I've been so rotten.

I tighten my fist and grit my teeth,
No purpose in life, like an empty sheath.

No place like you're your eyes, no place like your
heart.
And nothing but despair, whenever we're apart.

Reside in Me

A feeling has left me in a dark misty cloud.
Secluded we seem to the world, yet kiss
when no-one is around.

I cannot with-stand a contained feeling, a
contained love.
But I do realize the inevitable, when
push comes to shove.

Yet somewhere inside I feel that there is
a way, a chance for us.
To be happy for all our lives, and never
feel this lust.

I'd never ask a thing from you, it's your
life, your future, you decide.
But where you go, and what you do, this
love inside I feel for you,
Forever will reside.

Short and True

My baby and I,
we often cry,
when I 'm not at home,
and we're all alone.
It's then that I see,
How much she love's me.
And sometime's she's not sure.
But I tell you, I truly Love Her.

Smiles and Tears

With the days moving so fast,
and in a world where nothing can last.

It seems like all of what you felt has drifted away.
But I can clearly see, beyond what they say.

That you still love me and I still love you.
No matter what happens or what it is that you do.

I'll always be here, getting closer inside.
With the smiles, I've smiled, and the tears that I've cried.

Every last drop was worth it to me.
Because it's brought me here, where I want to be.

With you by my side, you whisper into my ears.
That I fill your life with love, and chase away your fears.

My love I see, the gestures you make.
And know that without me, your heart would surely break.

That where ever I am, you want to go.
So this I ask you, how much do you Love Me? I want to know!

So Alone

No matter how hard I try it's my heart that is always
crumbling.
And No matter how many times I pick myself up, I
always end up stumbling.

Left in a world with closed drapes, and a closed mind.
Left in this world alone, for all of time.

Is this what is to become of the person that is me.
Yet I love her still, can she really not see?

But I've already known that love goes two ways.
And now I feel nothing but abandonment, till the end
of my days.

Thank you oh lord, for sparing my soul.
And I hope there's someone out there. That'll make me
feel whole.

And I hope there is something you do, to take me out
of this hell.
That I feel for my love, my angel, my...Tinkerbelle.

So Cold

Like a blistering cold, a shiver does my spine feel.
I've been sick with a wicked infection.
A moon grows dark and the day seems all the more real.
When you're stuck by the needle of love's injection.

The sadness one relates overwhelms my day.
It is a lingering thought a lingering notion.
I search for a smile I search for a way.
To transform our heartache and accept love's potion.

It's connected our soul to one another.
Bound our hearts so that they may be one.
Yet when we're apart I weep, I shudder.
And when we're so close, the puzzle that is life will
then be done.

Something's Begun

Hold me close and never let go.

I Love you with all my heart, but you already know.

I keep on thinking of new ways to show.

And this feeling within continues to grow.

I see your smile, and it starts to glow.

I write these words to rhyme and flow.

And I'm left with sentences to reap and sow.

And I love you as sure, as the wind does blow.

Suspenseful Torture

Without knowing I know. Without saying I will say so much.
I love you to death and I long for your touch.

I know it'll be hard, but that's what Love is all about.
I want you to erase your fears, and erase your doubt.

Nothing will keep us apart, except for you.
I wonder every passing day, what will you do.

This feeling within me is ever so intense.
But I'm going crazy without you, cause I'm left in suspense.

Tell me you love me, I know that you do.
And I will forever, regardless of what you do.

I will be yours, there's nothing to fear.
But every second without you, it feels like a year.

I love you so much beautiful.

Sweet Memories

If you opened my heart, you know what you'd see.
Me holding you and you holding me.

Taking vacations, traveling the world with each other.
These are the memories that we'll share with one another.

If my life was a journal, you know what I'd write,
Stories of our, passionate nights.

And if my life was a magazine, would you subscribe?
You know I Love you in a way I could never describe.

But I know now how much it would hurt, to my surprise.
Yet you show me You Love Me, when I look into your eyes.

Tell Me

Tell me things that you'd like to do.
If I was right there, lying next to you.

Tell me about the hugs, that you'd smother me with.
Tell me you long, for my touch and my kiss.

Tell me that I am the one you dream of.
Tell me I'm the only one that you ever could love.

Tell me how much, you'd like to show.
That with only me, you'll let your heart go.

Tell me you miss me, in every way.
Tell me you'll love me, till your dying day.

That Lasts Forever

She is outgoing, and I am understanding,
I lift her up and yet I am never demanding.

So many times she's broken my heart,
And so many times, I've fallen apart.

When it seems so long, since I've heard her voice,
I feel I'm left to make a choice.

Should I continue to love and continue to fight?
For a chance to be with her, for only one more night.

Not the lust or passion of sin.
It's the joy and the sorrow that lingers within.

Yet I am here to hear her laugh.
Because I know this love forever will last.

This Girl

Raging inside when I think of you.
I want you to know, there's nothing I wouldn't do.

To hear you say that you love me.
Cause there's no other place that I'd rather be.

Help me to see, and open my eyes.
Enlighten my life, show me surprise.

Listen to our song, and what does it mean.
Look at my heart and watch it gleam.

Eternity to your heart is what I will bring.

Through It All

Through all of the tears, and all the times I've cried.
Through all the times I spoke the truth, when I know I
should have lied.

I'm still in love though I know I shouldn't be.
But, it's then with her, that I truly can see.

How wonderful love is, the smiles the laughter.
The thoughts of forever, and happily ever-after.

How hard it will be these years that lie ahead.
But years without you is a future I dread.

So at last I hope that you erase your fears, and erase
your doubt.
And realize that I am what you and you are what I,
cannot live without.

To The Lord I Pray

Thy love for me I compare to none.
And so happy am I, that her heart I've won.

Not that it is, just a prize to win.
But when we first met, I felt something within.

A glimmering hope, that this was love.
As I glanced at the clouds, and thanked my Lord above.

For never before, was I able to see.
This beautiful woman, that God sent to me.

So it's every evening, I now pray.
That I can receive, just one more day.

One more smile, one more kiss.
These are the things that I surely would miss.

Yet in slumber I sleep, and await the time.
When she holds me in her arms, and I hold her in mine.

What Do You Doubt

Do you doubt the love I feel, or fire in my eyes?
Or do you think the words I say are eternal lies.

Do you doubt the things I've said, or the things I'd do?
Or do you think there's someone else, other than you.

Do you doubt the time and the promises we share?
Or do you not believe that I will always care.

Do you doubt your feelings, doubt your love?
Or do you feel this doubt for no reason, just because.

Do you doubt your own desire, your own wishes?
Or do you regret our hugs, and regret our kisses.

Do you doubt that it will work, are you hesitant to try?
Or do you think that is won't, and for that reason you cry.

This existing doubt you feel, should never be.
Trust your heart, your love, and you will forever see.

Without Regret...Without Remorse

Forever without divorce,
And forever without remorse.

Are we still going to have it and give that to one
another?
And love like no other.

Are you hurting me because there is someone else
there?
Do you really not know how much I care?

The thought of you leaving me makes me feebly cry.
I stop and think and ask myself why.

Why do I let these tears flow down my cheeks?
Why does the sound of your voice make me feel so weak?

Some who read my letters that I write for you.
Say that they would kill to be in your shoes.

Funny it happens, to appear to me.
That at times you seem, not wanting to be.

But I'll never give up searching so far and searching
so wide.
And I'll never stop loving who you are inside.

Without Your Voice

I love the way, that you show me you care;
The smile on your face, and the wind in your hair.

Baby I know, that it should be plain to see;
All of this love, that's inside of me.

When I don't hear from you, it's then that I weep;
And I hope it's my heart that forever you keep.

So tell me now, and tell me true;
Whisper to me, "I'll Always Love You.".

Your Kiss and Your Hug

It's your voice that I miss;
Your hug and your kiss.
And I sit and ask myself why?

This heart in my shirt;
Does nothing but hurt.
Will you always be there, or did you just lie?

When I've opened up wide;
It's who you are inside.
That brushes the fear from my heart.

From the expressions of love;
Your kiss and your hug.
Has made me love you, from the very start.

The pain in my chest;
I'm losing my breath.
At the sound of your footsteps, walking away.

Do I not relieve?
Do you not believe?
That I'll love you now, till my dying day.

A crash of thunder;
That makes you shudder.
And lighting has clouded your mind.

Now it's plain to see;
That you'll always love me.
From now, till the end of time.

War...
(25 poems of patriotism and sacrifice)

A Change of Life

Whether your black, white, yellow or green;
We're always looking for more on our team.

You can fight, learn, and get paid too;
If you'll always stand by, the red white and blue.

You'll see much more, than your hearts desire;
And we'll fill your body with a raging fire.

A fire to be, the best that you can;
We'll mold you in, to a whole new man.

And when you get out, you'll carry the pride;
And no one can change, who you are inside.

A Fighting Hole

My buddy and me are stuck in a hole,
Sittin and waitin, just chewin our skoal.

Nine to twelve, and twelve to three,
I cover his back as he does for me.

Inside we wonder are we scared or ready,
And hope our fingers, and aim are steady.

Faith in me and faith in him,
Is how I know that we will win.

Together there's nothing that we couldn't do.
So watch your step, we're waiting for YOU.

A Nation that Stands

A battlefield cry, throughout the land;
That shakes the ground, every woman and man.

It comes from a beast, or so it seems;
Oh no it's worse, it's the U.S. Marines.

Run for your life, is heard throughout;
Or we'll be shot from 500 out.

They covered the ground, the sea and skies;
Until all of the enemy, submits or dies.

And what's left standing, so high and tall;
The American Colors, the brightest of all.

An Eagle Above

A soaring Eagle, above our head,
Reminds us all, of the blood we've shed.

A soaring Eagle over the car we bought,
Reminds us of, the battles we've fought.

A soaring Eagle above our homes,
Reminds us all of courage we've shown.

A soaring Eagle within our lives,
We think of a Marine, who fights and dies.

A soaring Eagle above our land,
Means freedom and peace, and United We Stand.

Bleeding Together

The title Marine is what makes me true;
And gladly die for the red white and blue.

With honor and courage throughout our lives;
We've shown commitment and carried our pride.

We've bled in combat, for love within;
And we'd proudly do, the same again.

We're set so high above the rest;
A love so strong, you can't contest.

There is no end to the ongoing war;
No end to freedom, No end to Corps.

Brothers That Weep

A crash of thunder and a bolt of lightning.
Never has green, ever looked more frightening.

But at the sight of a rifle, yes M16.
Causes a shudder right down to your spleen.

Who's to explain the tears that were cried?
And who's to explain, how a warrior has died.

One fought and died for the preservation of life.
It's the burden of his brothers that carry this strife.

Yet they fight on for their family now gone.
To ensure that freedom, lives on and on.

Called Upon

Here we stand a band of brothers.
We cover our six and watch each other's.

Our weapon on hand right by our side.
Leaving no place for the wretched to hide.

We fly in quick and stay there long.
To make things right and banish the wrong.

My job is simple, to defend and kill.
The love for my country, gives me the will.

Go anywhere, when you're called to bleed.
You'd do the same if you were me.

Accomplish the mission without any gripes.
And give your life, for the stars and stripes.

Departed

A rising sun, a fallen man;
How much more will our country withstand.

A mighty warrior, a shallow foe;
A lowly tear that drowns below.

Departing soon, return unknown;
Thankless deeds, of bravery shown.

A forgotten struggle, a thousand stairs;
Yet high above, are thoughts and prayers.

And so embark, on an unknown task.
With Honor inside, that forever will last.

Draped in Honor

Draped in red at rest he is.
His life nothing more than a whisper in the wind.

So long he trained, his life seemingly forgotten subsides.
Yet never by his brother who carries his memory of
spirit inside.

Courage he wavered on a battlefield so far.
And lost his life in the perseverance of ours.

So hard to believe, what so many do not know.
About the dangerous places that we're happy to go.

For just one chance to do what many would only dream of.
To show how much, their country is loved.

Draped in honor and in eternal despair.
Is the burden of life, which all Marines share.

End of Days

With guns, ammo and so much more,
We're standing by to fight for Corps.

Armed inside with strength and power,
Until it comes our dying hour.

But even then, it's seen throughout,
The Marine inside, isn't taken out.

Not done for the money, but all for the thrill.
With strength to lead, and desire to kill.

And so we stand, till the end of days,
Or all of the enemy, on the ground thus lays.

Forever Remembered

Running and shouting, can't wait to get in;
I can hear the colors, start to begin.

It's just begun; it's not too late;
Quick inside, or we'll have to wait.

And he who stays will always know;
To stand so tall, when colors blow.

Forever remembered those who have died;
And all of the families, who've lost and cried.

It's never forgotten, by those who have stayed;
Even when the very last note, of colors is played.

Forgotten

Pistol Grips, hand guards, front sight posts.
These are the things that I love the most.

Some days I get tired, and am all alone.
Yet here in the Corps I've found a home.

Kevlar, pack, and my warrior stance.
Equipped with these, they won't stand a chance.

Cammi's, Service, and don't forget Dress.
Is why we're set, above the rest.

Forgotten, lost, or become astray.
Just look to the Marines and you'll find your way.

It's Done for You

Cold and alone, day after day.
A Marine and his rifle, on the ground thus lay.

Awaiting a signal or some kind of sign,
That secretly tells them, it's almost that time.

A time to turn or time to fight,
As soon as the enemy is within our sight.

Cross hairs on point and ready to squeeze.
To bring his mark down to his knees.

The life of a Marine is bitter but true.
It's not done for pleasure, but all for you.

Just One

Armed with a musket, one round at a time,
No flak and no Kevlar, but that was just fine.

Awaiting the first of the battles to start.
We charged into war, with only our heart.

It took only one, of our Marines to fight,
And victory was near and within our sight.

We still fought on even if shot,
Cause we fought with our spirits, and they did not.

Outnumbered by thousands, and still we won,
With only one round, and only one gun.

Liberty

Explosions and rounds, whizzing by your face;
You ask yourself how, did you get in this place.

You're stuck in a hole, some six feet down;
And look to your buddy, who's asleep on the ground.

You shake his shoulder and try to speak;
Wake up You Fool; it's my turn to sleep.

And so you rotate, day in and day out;
Until you're awoken by a very loud shout.

Run Men, it's going to be great.
The formation for LIBO, where nobody's late.

Marines of the Past

Many Marines, have fought and died;
And those who live on have carried the pride.

For a battle be it close or ever so far;
It's next to impossible to forget who we are.

If it weren't for us, we wouldn't be loved,
We wouldn't be feared;
And might be run over, by a man with a beard.

So if you're alone and tired, hungry or cold;
Just think of the past and remember the old.

They once did fight, and bled for you;
They died in war, to let freedom ring true.

Power of Marines

A Marine alone has the power inside,
To make his voice heard far and wide.

The power to defeat with strength to lead,
The will to die, and ability to bleed.

To hold a rifle ever so close,
And fight and die for what matters most.

A freedom so long, that we have held,
It's forged from steel that had to be weld.

A Marine always knows what we stand for,
A Band of Brothers, that we call the Corps.

Prints

I stepped on those prints, and so did you;
But at that time, nobody knew.

Someday we'd forget what they did hate;
That selfishness inside that they tried to break.

On your face, your feet, and face again.
It seemed no matter what, we never would win.

Then somewhere between double and time;
Something within, had begun to shine.

The feeling of love yet even more;
The feeling of pride when I joined the Corps.

Put me on Patrol

If you see the enemy while out on patrol;
Don't Shoot, yet. Maintain control.

Sneak up close, get right beside;
Don't make a sound when you rack the slide.

Get close enough, but don't let him see;
One shot one kill, that's all there should be.

When you see him fall and hit the weeds;
Spit on his corpse and watch him bleed.

Mission accomplished and you'd humbly kill more.
To defend your family, country, and corps.

(This is in no way true about the conductivity of military operations)

Restless Silence

We push ourselves to that next step;
Within our hearts, our sorrow's kept.

Below raging sea and above rolling sky;
Are Marines and Sailors who fight and die.

For our fallen comrades we can't forget;
And deep inside our tears are wept.

They gave it all, every ounce they had;
They bled for their Country, and they were glad.

Restless and silent, on and on;
As WE fight and die, for those who are gone.

Sacrifice

I was once told a story, that I once knew;
Of a Marine in battle, just like you.

A brave man indeed and still it is shown;
How respect for our past, and honor have grown.

Who is this man that I speak of;
A man with a mission, with only one love.

He was awarded the highest medal allowed;
From the spirit he had that made him proud.

He led his troops to the center of war;
And gave his life, for his brothers in Corps.

Terrorism

The Man that hides and Quivers at our Sight

Wave less seas, and blue less skies
Is a perfect world in the devil's eyes.

A blackened mist throughout the land
To destroy us all, with a single hand.

This devil of ours that has no end.
Will tempt "his" fate with evil again.

And here we'll be firm and steady
Our forces are strong, and at the ready.

So devil you are, and devil you'll stay
Within your lair till you're old and grey.

Unknown Death

A Fallen Comrade

A man walks, lingering alone.
Overcome by discipline, still it is shown.

Always needing more.
Engulfed, perished, for his Corps.

Abrupt.

A family now weeps, over their loss.
At what cost?

Unknown to the world without any cares.
The memories that were his, a family shares.

A loss often unspoken to those who would
otherwise be oblivious.

Perhaps now they can know.
The pain of a family and experience their woe.

What It's All About

My Brothers and I

It's not what you think, or what you say you do;
It's about the millions of People which look up to you.

It's not about strength or the fear in your eyes;
It's about the spirit and the heart that's inside.

It's not about what you have, but what you can give;
It's about what you do, so others can live.

It's not about what you want, or things that you need;
It's about the sweat that you pour and the blood that you bleed.

It's not what you say or things that you know;
It's about the love that you have, and the love that you show.

Where are You

You sit and dream of total world peace.
You sit and dream of a house with no lease.

Dreams that we have that perhaps come true,
Are reasons we fight for the red, white, and blue.

A new day a new mission, we constantly strive.
To keep the hopes and dreams of millions alive.

When I closed my eyes, its then I could see.
That throughout this world there's more than just me.

I know what I do and the person I am.
Do you know who you are, and where it is that you stand?

Miscellaneous...
(8 poems)

A Mother With Endless Love

Dedicated to my Mother

A mother holds a dying rose to her bosom.
Gently she shakes it in hope of awakening.
Sadly the rose just whittles.
Weeping...
She calms herself by breathing softly.
Suddenly the rose begins blooming.
She's learned a lesson from this rose.
Never relinquish a glimpse of diminishing hope.
In hopes that she will always look for her roses to bloom.

We Love You, and will all Bloom for you when our season is
near.

This Life

I gaze into the night.
I see stars that shine so bright.
Emptiness surrounds me.
Blinded, and I cannot see.
Weeping...
And the clouds that broke are peeking.
Oblivious to future.
Overcome by shadow, overcome with this strife.
Yet I am able to cope, accepting life.
**
As I realize what paths I am able to take I accept what is real.

A Light in the Darkness

To those whom are lost in darkness, there is hope.

Anguished by all, pain throughout;
In a black abyss a shuddering shout.

Banished below a thousand floors,
to every room;
A glimmering light, a hope, beneath the
doors of darkened doom.

Time elapses a changing world to light;
To rid our eyes of misty shade,
and brighten up this night.

Hope is yours to embrace, do not despair;
The light inside your soul is yours,
to forever share.

So rejoice the light in you, it may not
be much;
And spread the warmth, in every thing
you touch.

I Pray

A prayer I recite below stars so bright,
And I speak this prayer every single night.

Guide me lord to a place of peace and serenity.
Oh holy one, keep me from losing, my sanity.

Show me that this love within, was given by you.
And guide me in the decisions I make and things that I do.

Divert this lustrous imagination into that of purity.
I request this love this happiness, this security.

Oh gracious one and heavenly host.
It is the name of the lord, and the love within;
That I love the most.

A Passing Day

I close me heavy eyes,
Like a curtain that comes crashing down.
Darkness surrounds me.
I scramble for some air.
Suffocating
The passage to my lungs have closed.
Blind I am,
Air is gone, I begin to slip.
Into oblivion unable to see, unable to breathe.
What is one to do when the fate you fear dangles before you.
Like fly caught in a spider's web.
Continue to fight I was once told.

A Seedling

A mound of dirt upon the ground.
The peasant did look and began to frown.

How indeed will I accomplish wealth?
A seedling to start, he said to himself.

I'll plant a seed and watch it grow.
I'll show it love and teach it to glow.

To shine so bright and grow really tall.
And to pick yourself up when you inevitably fall.

Wow do I build, a long wooden shelf.
A seedling to start, he thought to himself.

Bleeding Sun

In the eyes of an angel lays a picture of beauty.
A fragile place where birds flutter under a bleeding sun.
This pours hope towards the people lost in their
lives.
Searching for the truth within their hearts they are
blind.
Guided only by the light provided by the illuminant
sun.
So lead astray are they by this bleeding sun.
As they search for a book which contains no answers. Only tears.
I beseech upon you, look towards the caverns of your
heart.
You will find a brightness that can not be described,
as here I feebly shall attempt.
The light within our souls is that of love;
And how glamorous does its rays shine.
Ever so bright, which cloud our decisions.
We sacrifice our lives for its preservation, for its
continuation, for its existence.
For this love, we give our all, we give our tears.
To rid this blood that shades our sun, we give our
lives.

Writing

To Those whom are in the need for an extra nudge to create

Pen to paper and paper to pen,
And the literary mind starts to bend.

Creativity and imagination begin to spill.
It's the hope of sharing that gives us a thrill.

The will to open and pour out our mind.
In hope that we create, a one-of-a-kind.

Magnificent and beautiful, the work is displayed.
As we hope our reader, understands the message
portrayed.

An eternal mark how can we show.
Just open your mind, and let the words just flow.